D0783738

FIVE ESCAPE
BREXIT ISLAND

Other adventures in this series:

Enid Blyton

FIVE ESCAPE BREXIT ISLAND

Text by
Bruno Vincent

Enid Blyton for Grown-Ups

Quercus

First published in Great Britain in 2017 by

Quercus Editions Ltd
Carmelite House
50 Victoria Embankment
London EC4Y 0DZ

An Hachette UK company

A CIP catalogue record for this book is available
from the British Library

ISBN 978 1 78648 698 1

Text by Bruno Vincent
Original illustrations by Eileen A. Soper
Cover illustration by Ruth Palmer

10 9 8 7 6 5 4

Typeset by CC Book Production

Printed and bound in Great Britain by Clays Ltd, St Ives plc

Contents

CHAPTER ONE

Julian Stands Firm

It was a time for hard negotiations. And Julian felt up to the task. Cometh the hour, he told himself, cometh the Julian.

'Now, listen here,' he said. 'There's more at stake than pounds and pence. This is about decency, and human rights, and a good old-fashioned British – *British*, I say – sense of fair play. So remove this pettifogging demand and come back with something reasonable, and perhaps we can talk!'

The man he was addressing was aghast. His mouth hung open.

'Perhaps you weren't expecting to be addressed in this way,' said Julian. 'Well, I cannot help it. I am a man of passion and I stand up for my beliefs!' Rather pleased with this peroration, he looked around, half expecting to be greeted with applause. When he turned back, the man had recovered his powers of speech.

'Listen, mate,' he said. 'If you want an the Megacoach

Turbo-thrift Hypersaver tarrif, you have to book online in advance. It's as simple as that. There's no point arguing about it. Look, there's a queue building up; I'm going to have to ask you to pay or let me serve another customer.'

Julian was outraged. However much he would have liked to stay and debate British values with this fiend in human shape, he couldn't overlook the fact that one of the most profound of those values was respect for the sanctity of a queue.

'Fine,' he said, brandishing his debit card.

'If you could just pop your PIN number into the machine for me.'

'It is not a PIN *number*,' Julian said. 'It is a *PIN*! "PIN number" is grossly tautological!' There were loud groans all the way down the queue as Julian tapped it in. 'And I'm a *passenger*, not a customer,' he said, snatching the ticket off the counter.

'Very good, sir,' said the man behind the counter. 'You have a pleasant journey, now.'

'*Why* must you make such a scene?' Anne asked when he joined the others by the coach door. 'You are so un*utterably* horrible sometimes, Julian.'

He made to reply, but she stopped him.

'So unBritish!' he said to the others, when he returned.
'There's not an atom of fair play in that thoroughgoing
rotter, from his quiff to his toenails!'

'I don't want to hear it,' Anne said. 'You can jolly well keep your mouth shut until we get to Dorset, thank you.'

George returned from the coach station's coffee concession with lattes and croissants.

'Didn't get any of that foreign muck for Billy Big Bollocks,' she said, nodding at Julian. 'Thought it might interfere with his British values. Hey, Anne, I never really asked. Why are we going to Dorset this time?'

'Well,' Anne said. 'I'll explain . . .'

Anne, George, Dick, Timmy the dog and Julian were all on their way to Dorset to visit their cousin Rupert and his wife, Anastasia, but, much more importantly, they were going to see Rupert and Anastasia's daughter, Lily.

Rupert was a businessman with a wide range of interests, nearly all of which were nefarious to some greater or lesser degree. It just so happened that, one year earlier, having yet again aroused the curiosity of law enforcement, he and his wife had spent a brief period behind bars.

During these few months, the care of their precious baby daughter, then just six months old, had passed to the next of kin – this had been Rupert's cousins Anne, George *et al.* – and, of course, a deep attachment had formed.

In the year since, it had been almost impossible to see Lily, as Rupert always seemed to be dashing off with his family to far-flung places, to explore business deals, evade tax, or give the body-swerve to another extradition treaty.

Finally, though, an invitation had come. And as they caught the coach south, their hearts warmed at the prospect of seeing her again.

'I remember her sweet little smile,' said Anne.

'And the way her tiny hand held on to my little finger,' said Dick.

Even George smiled at this revelation of Dick's softer, more fatherly side.

'I remember her doing a liquid poo all over my P. G. Wodehouse hardbacks,' said Julian.

'No one said you could talk,' said Anne.

'Woof!' agreed Timmy.

CHAPTER TWO

Reunion

When they were led into the living room of the Dorset cottage, there was Anastasia sitting on the edge of the sofa, Lily's hands gripping her mother's forefingers, and her pudgy face locked in a sort of benign puzzlement as she plonked one foot in front of the other. Anastasia was beaming.

'She's WALKING!' screamed Anne.

The noise of this was much too much for Lily, who immediately fell on to her nappy-clad bum and started to cry. Anne was distraught, but Anastasia shushed her.

'Don't be silly,' she said. 'Babies cry – that's what they do. Now, all of you sit down, and let me fetch you a drink.'

'Whisky,' said Julian, without thinking. 'Or, you know, white wine? What time is it?'

'I was thinking tea or coffee,' said Anastasia. 'It's half eleven.'

A deal was struck where Dick, Anne and George were

served tea, and Rupert, who had picked the guests up from the station, and presently returned from parking the car, served himself and Julian a small pre-lunch snifter.

'Do you remember who this is?' Anastasia asked Lily, plonking her on Dick's lap.

'Smelly uncle,' said Lily.

'Hah! It's as though I trained her,' said Julian.

'She was looking at you,' said Anne.

'All of us are uncles, aren't we, darling girl, except Anne?' George asked, stealing Lily and bouncing her up and down on her knee. 'She doesn't suck her feet as much as she did,' she observed. 'God, she's heavier, though. And prettier. If that's possible. Which I didn't think it could be. Did I? No, I didn't!'

George was temporarily lost in the enormous eyes looking defencelessly up at her, and the shy smile that accompanied them, and had become uncharacteristically gooey. 'I think your favourite uncle is Uncle George, isn't that right? Yes? Uncle George is best?'

Julian found the glass in his hand empty, and gave Rupert a casual glance of enquiry, followed by several clearings of the throat, which his cousin effortlessly ignored.

'So how does it feel to have the most adorable baby in

Julian decided that, if he couldn't communicate
with the guards verbally, he would find another way
to make himself understood.

the history of everything?' Anne asked, when she had Lily to herself.

'Exhausting, annoying and wonderful, I suppose,' said Rupert, giving one of his lizard smiles, albeit one which tended ever so slightly more than usual towards the human. 'What would you say, darling?'

Anastasia came in from the kitchen.

'I would say lunch is ready,' she said, 'and I want some bums on seats in here.'

After lunch, they all agreed that, on such a beautiful autumn day, it would be criminal not to go for a walk along the cliffs. Lily was hoisted onto Dick's shoulders, where she happily sung, squawked and tugged at his mop of dark hair. Dick gently chuckled, gripping her legs and making them kick in rhythm to a song of his own devising.

The Channel was a murky blue-grey, shot with occasional dazzling patches of gold where the sun burst through the scurrying clouds. The wind buffeted them, making Lily scream with excitement, and taking snatches of conversation away with it, while the long grass whipped around their ankles.

'What was that?' Rupert asked for the third time.

'I said, what happened to your *island*?' Anne yelled.

'Don't you remember?' George asked. 'Last year, during the Brexit kerfuffle . . .'

'Kerfuffle' was a particularly unhelpful word to use, as it was indistinguishable from the sound of the wind in their ears. Rupert, growing frustrated, directed them to a more sheltered path down the cliff edge.

When she mentioned Rupert's 'island', Anne was referring to the dramatic events of the previous summer, after the Brexit referendum. The four adventurers (five, including Timmy) had been camping on Kirrin Island in Dorset when the referendum result was announced, and, in a fit of temper, George had declared Kirrin Island independent of Britain.

It had been a disaster. The press had descended, and a further referendum among the five of them had threatened to break them up forever.

The one beneficiary was Rupert, who had just inherited a chunk of nearby coast. He perceived that there was a lot of money to be made by creating a tiny independent island state that could offer tax-exempt status to international conglomerates. He had moved heaven and earth (although more earth than heaven – several thousand tonnes, to be exact) to turn one corner of his property into an island.

The four housemates had heard nothing of the project since.

Now, as they all inched carefully down the cliff path (Dick especially so), and the wind receded enough to allow conversation, they expected Rupert to explain. But, instead, one by one, they all noticed that he was just standing ahead of them on the path, and pointing.

'Cripes!' said Anne, desperately trying not to swear.

'Jesus Christ painting watercolours!' said George.

'Fungus the Bogeyman!' said Julian.

'Fuck me!' said Dick. 'Oops – er, sorry, Lily.'

'Smelly uncle,' said Lily.

'Woof!' Timmy agreed.

CHAPTER THREE

The Fortress of Solitude

'It's so bleak,' said Anne.

'It's terrifying!' said Dick.

'Ghoulish,' said George.

'I *love* it,' said Julian.

Before them stood a stone construction that more than lived up to all of their adjectives. From the grassy clifftop, far above their heads, down to the waves crashing on the shingle below, a steep triangular gully of some hundred feet or more had been gouged into the cliff, leaving an enormous chunk of earth on its own man-made little island.

What took their breath away, however, was the stone fortress which perched on that lump of rock.

'We knew there were some stone ruins when we started digging,' said Rupert. 'But we had no idea it was anything like this. It was thought to have collapsed or been destroyed back in the fourteenth century, at the same time as many of the local villages disappeared due to plague. But it seems it just fell into disuse and ruin. In those days, it was a quarter of a mile inland. Once we'd uncovered it, I saw what a tourist trap I had. Think of the money to be made!'

'So your plans for getting Apple and Starbucks and so on to relocate here for tax purposes came to naught?' George asked.

'Negotiations broke down,' Rupert admitted, 'once they realized that they'd actually have to maintain an office here, and that it would be in a ... er ... well ...'

They all looked again at the battlements, which were truly fearsome.

'Let's take a peek, then!' said Dick. 'Shall we go to prison, Lily?'

'Pizzun!' Lily cried. Rupert stepped on to the wooden footbridge that led across to the gates.

'WHO DARES ENTER?' boomed a voice over their heads.

Julian, Anne, George and Dick all quailed. Lily squealed with delight.

Rupert also laughed and, at the pressing of a button on his keyring, there was a high-pitched *blip-blip* sound, and the portcullis started to rise.

'It cost a fair few quid to have this reinstalled,' Rupert

said, 'with all the parts made in the original style. But the effect should be suitably chilling to visitors, when we open in the New Year.'

'I'll say,' said Julian, as the castle gate yawned above him. 'It chills the blood.'

'And does something unpleasant to the stomach,' said Dick, looking up at the black iron blades, each as wide as a shovel and as thick as a George R. R. Martin paperback. 'Unless that's you, Lily,' he said, waggling her legs. 'Have you done a stinky?'

'NO!' shouted Lily.

'Okay, that's enough,' said Rupert. 'I think I'll take her back now, thank you. You have a look around while I close the portcullis, to give you the full experience. I'll go up to the office and try to show you all the bells and whistles. They should be online by now. I think you'll be impressed.'

As the points of the portcullis juddered towards their holes in the ground, accompanied by a hideous metallic squeaking, the group felt as though they'd been transported back in time. In the autumnal light, it was a fearful place, the sky above them delineated by the castellations, and shadows swelling in the corners.

'It's so cool,' said George. 'So, so cool.'

'Escape first, talk about politics later!' said George.

'Utterly chilling,' said Anne. 'Imagine being trapped here.'

'What's that sound?' said Julian.

They all looked up at a glass booth above the gate. Inside, they could see Rupert, well lit, with Lily on his shoulders. There was a popping noise in the courtyard, and then they could hear Rupert's voice.

'Yes, darling,' he was saying, in response to an indecipherable low-level warble that could be heard in the background. 'We'll go home soon. Now, be quiet for Daddy, because I have to let those little bas— Oh. Has this been on all along?'

He seemed suddenly to notice that the four housemates were looking up at him. They all nodded.

'Right. So, if you look to your left, you should see a rather grisly film of medieval dungeon practices, projected on the wall there.'

They looked around them, left and right, north and south, but could see only encroaching darkness.

'Press the button again!' Julian yelled. He saw that, in the booth above, Rupert was chatting to his daughter and smiling. 'He can't bloody hear us,' he said. 'Let's wave.' They jumped up and down as they did so, and, after a few seconds, caught their cousin's attention.

'Nothing doing?' called the voice over the tannoy. 'Oh, this is silly of me. I should have waited until our opening weekend, rather than doing this on my o—' His voice disappeared with a squeak.

The shadows in the castle courtyard had now risen above the prisoners' heads, turning into a dark soup that was enveloping them completely.

'What's he playing at?' Anne asked. Behind the glass, they could see their cousin pressing lots of buttons on the controls and yelling into a microphone, but no sound came out to them.

'I'm so sorry,' he said through the PA at last. He looked frazzled, and Lily was wailing in the background. 'I don't know what's happened. Something terrible has gone wrong with the electricity. I'll have it fixed shortly. I'm so terribly sorry.'

'Don't apologize,' said George, although she knew he couldn't hear them. 'It's not like you're going to leave us here . . .'

'And Lily's definitely done a . . . Well, she needs a change. I think the thing is to get her home straight away, and ring for support. But I'll be back shortly, I *promise* . . .'

'SON OF A BITCH!' George screamed. Even if her

scream had been ten times louder, Rupert, in his soundproof booth, would still not have heard it. Instead, it rose up to the sky and dissipated uselessly in the evening air, having no effect other than leaving Anne temporarily deaf. The others all called out with their own expressions of anger and disbelief, none any more effective than George's.

'Woof!' protested Timmy, 'Woof, woof!'

CHAPTER FOUR

Back in the Jug Agane

'When will he be back?' Anne asked. 'What does he mean by this?'

The others didn't bother to answer. Instead, they looked around at the unforgiving environment and wondered what dangers it might pose, other than the obvious ones – exposure, starvation and fright.

'Do you think we're here for the night, then?' Dick asked.

'Seems likely,' said Julian. 'I'd like to say I don't believe it, but, if you think about it, it's completely in line with his previous behaviour . . .'

'Oh, don't be silly,' said Anne. 'It's just a hiccup. I'm sure he feels perfectly awful about it. The last thing we should do is worry . . .'

There was something particularly unpleasant about the way Anne's words echoed back at them out of the darkness. She shivered.

19

'Let's find somewhere to keep warm,' said George. 'Down here, perhaps . . .'

The others, alarmed that they couldn't see her, followed her voice. They found themselves stumbling down a stone staircase, then turning at the bottom towards the light of her mobile phone.

'The *dungeon*,' whispered Dick.

As they explored with the light of their smartphones, they soon found that the dungeons were littered with cheap, gimmicky plastic props. If they had felt up to a discussion about it, they would surely have agreed that these props, although no doubt laughable during the day, were a lot less amusing by torchlight.

They stumbled first across an upright suit of armour wielding an axe, then a stand of inventively nasty-looking instruments of torture and (a few feet further into the darkness) an apparently fully operational rack – unoccupied, for the time being.

These were followed by a skeleton with its hands chained in manacles to the walls. The skeleton was wearing the rags of a cloth shirt, which George decided to remove and place round Anne's shoulders. To free up her hands for this procedure, however, George put her phone between her

'Tally ho, my hearties!' cried Julian, as they pushed
away from the rocks. 'Shit! Is it supposed to do that?'

teeth, and the irritatingly flexible skeleton put up such a fight while she wrestled with it that the dungeon became illuminated by a flickering nightmare, reminiscent of the less relaxing scenes in *The Blair Witch Project.*

'Sorry,' George said at length, when the light had stopped flashing around the room. But everyone was too spooked to accept her apology.

There were a few slit windows through which they could see that dusk had come and gone, and a bright moon hung low in the sky. They decided that this corner of the dungeon was, in all likelihood, no more damp, cold and unpleasant than anywhere else to be found. They might as well rest here for the time being.

Julian retraced their steps up to the courtyard again, to see if there was any sign of their cousin. But he knew there wouldn't be, and he was right. Not so much as an apology scrawled on a handkerchief, pinned to the fletch of an arrow and fired into the keep, which Julian thought was the least he would have done, in the same position, It was yet another beastly betrayal by that craven delinquent.

'So un*British*!' he said to the others, when he returned. 'There's not an atom of fair play in that thoroughgoing rotter, from his quiff to his toenails!'

It's not a quiff, Anne thought; it's more of a wave. But she didn't have the energy to reply. They were all leaning on each other's shoulders and nodding off, with Timmy lying across their laps.

They awoke to the sound of tapping, and to the sight of Julian walking up and down the inner wall, knocking his phone against bricks.

'Oh, God,' said Anne, realizing where she was.

'I can't believe we're in prison,' said Dick, sitting up and groaning. 'And we didn't even have the fun of doing anything wrong.'

'Well, I think it's romantic,' said Julian. 'It's a puzzle, a challenge. How often in life are we given something like this to fight against? Imagine if we actually succeed in escaping!'

'I'm all up for escaping,' said Dick, 'but only after breakfast.'

'Where's your backbone?' Julian asked.

'It's behind my stomach,' said Dick.

'Don't talk rot,' said Anne. 'Rupert will be back first thing to let us out. We know he will.'

'With all due love and respect, Anne,' George said, 'you're talking crap. That bastard's always up to something.

'It is not a *PIN* number,' *Julian said.* 'It is a PIN!
"*PIN number*" *is grossly tautological!*'

We're in here for a reason, I'll bet. And I don't intend to find out what it is. Julian, what the bloody hell *are* you doing?'

'Tapping the bricks,' he said.

'We can see that,' said Anne. 'But why, please?'

'To find a secret compartment, of course,' said Julian. 'Castles like this are full of secret passageways and priest holes and treasure troves and whatnot. Don't you two remember *anything* from the old days?'

'Oh dear,' said George.

'Yes, I know,' said Anne. 'He's finally gone mad.'

'Not that,' said George. 'You remember when we were looking after Lily, and Rupert was in prison?'

'Yes?' said Dick.

'I'd forgotten that it was us who put him there.'

'Ah,' said Dick. 'Yes, I think I had, too.'

'This is his revenge,' said George.

'You mean he'll just leave us here to rot?' asked Anne. 'Surely that's—'

But Anne was cut off by a sound that caught their attention. The last stone Julian had tapped made a distinctly different sound from all the preceding ones. All the regular stones produced a quiet, solid click. But this one made a much more satisfyingly hollow sound that echoed inwards.

'Bloody hell – I didn't expect to hit gold that fast,' said Julian.

Dick came and squatted next to him, and together they knocked on the surrounding stones until they had identified a roughly suitcase-sized hollow panel near the floor.

'I'll bet it's a fireplace,' said Julian. 'You know, in old castles like this, the fireplaces used t—' He was cut off by a thundering crash as George kicked the panel in with one of her heavy boots.

'History lesson later; extreme violence first,' she said.

The panel was made of thin plywood, painted over (rather hastily, they now saw) to look like the surrounding stonework. With a few supplementary kicks, George took care of the rest of the panel, and she and Dick stuck their heads in to look.

'Seems he's right,' said George. 'It is a fireplace, and the chimney extends down to the floor below. And look! There's light down there. It could be a way out!'

'Woof!' said Timmy.

'Bagsy I go down to try it out first,' said Dick.

'Oh, do be careful,' said Anne. 'What if you can't get back up?'

'Back up here?' George asked. 'Into the imprisoning bit of the prison?'

Anne nodded. Sometimes she spoke without thinking.

George had already taken off her belt, and she put out her hand for Dick's and Julian's too. Then she tied them together, pulled hard to make sure they held, and gave one end to Dick.

'Okay, here goes,' he said. He squeezed backwards through the gap, then his voice was echoing up the chimney. 'God, I've missed this sort of thing. Okay, so I'm down. Oh! Hello. So sorry to bother . . .'

Anne gasped.

George looked up at her. 'He's found someone!'

'I think you should come down and look at this,' Dick said.

'Woof,' said Timmy quietly, looking at the others.

CHAPTER FIVE

From the Frying Pan into a Slightly different Frying Pan

One by one, they all scrambled down, George insisting on going last, with Timmy clinging to her back. The others tried to argue, but she pointed out that the final person had to descend without the assistance of the belt rope, and she was by far the most practised rock climber. When she'd tumbled out of the hole below, got up and dusted herself down, George was face to face with a rather tall, pale man wearing glasses and a bright yellow jumpsuit. They were all standing in a small, low cell, with morning sunshine pouring in through the open doorway.

'Um,' she said. 'I hope you don't mind us popping in like this.'

Before the man could speak, another appeared in the doorway. He yelped and called for others to come and see. Then he came back to stare at the newcomers.

'What are the chances?' said George, pointing from one

bright yellow jumpsuit to the other. 'Matching outfits. How embarrassing.'

'Don't worry about that,' said the second man. 'How did you get in? Does that mean there's a way *out* of this place?'

'I don't know if you'd want to climb back up there,' said Julian, pointing at the fireplace they had just exited. 'Besides, it's just a horrible prison.'

The first man looked suddenly as though a weight was on his shoulders – the expression of one to whom it falls to break bad news. He led them to the doorway. They all gasped.

'Oh, shit,' said Dick.

Timmy, rather than say 'woof', gulped.

These two men, the first to have greeted the Kirrins, acted proprietorially about their new guests, as though they had first dibs, and told all the others, who gathered round as they came out into the yard, to back off and give them room. But everyone was deeply interested to hear what the Kirrins had to say, and to hear news of the outside world.

George, Dick, Anne and Julian found themselves surrounded by around forty men in identical yellow jumpsuits.

They were all white, in varying degrees of middle age, and looked exhausted.

The pale man, for instance, introduced himself as a lecturer in journalism at the University of Coventry, called Jim Clarke.

'I'm sure you'll be able to get out of here very soon,' he reassured them. 'Not us, though. We're in here for the long haul. Don't know our own legal status; don't know nothing.'

Anne, who had fainted upon seeing what amounted to a prison yard, was still being tended to by George and Dick. But Julian was getting a good look at the detention centre in which they suddenly found themselves.

This back part of the castle, which had been invisible from the front, was lower and deeper, and its walls tall – rising more than sixty feet above them and topped with loops of barbed wire. Each corner of the motte (or bailey, Julian wasn't sure which) had been converted into a lookout, manned by men holding automatic weapons, and with enormous searchlights, ready for use.

Dotted around the walls of the central area were further guards, all huge, fearsome-looking men with thousand-yard stares.

'What *is* this place?' Julian asked.

'Don't joke, Rupert,' said Julian. 'I like a joke as much as the next man. More, perhaps.' He thought for a moment. 'No, about the same, actually.'

'Doesn't have a name,' said Jim. 'Officially, I don't think it exists.'

'So . . .' Julian was stumped for a follow-up question. 'But it's a prison of some sort, right?'

'Certainly feels like one,' Jim said. 'I think it's a prototype – for the detention centres they want to set up after Brexit is finished. Protecting the borders from illegal immigrants, you know. But keeping them off British soil, so the laws don't apply and they can do what they please – like Guacamoleo.'

'You mean Guantanamo,' said Julian. There was an instant hush across the courtyard.

'Try not to say that word, would you?' said one bloke from a nearby group, whose heated argument had suddenly fallen silent. 'It's not good for morale.'

'But hang on – why would a lecturer from Coventry be detained by Immigration?' asked Julian. 'What are you being charged with? Surely *you* weren't trying to get into Britain by illicit means?'

Jim shrugged.

'I wasn't trying to get *into* the country,' said the second man. 'My name's Giles Reardon Smith. I'm an archaeologist. I was trying to get *out*.'

'Really?'

He nodded. 'I'd just accepted a job at the University of Hamburg. I reckon the government's trying to prevent the great post-Brexit brain-drain. We're all academics, here. There's Jamie Coleman, a noted Proctologist, head-hunted by Erasmus University Hospital in Rotterdam. Joe Hoff, a world expert in sports physiotherapy – he'd just been poached away from working with the England squad by AC Milan. We were all trying to take jobs abroad.'

'But this – this – this is . . .' Julian spluttered.

'An outrage?' Jim Clarke asked.

'Well, yes!'

None of the Kirrin adventurers could bear an injustice, and here was one that could serve as a dictionary definition.

So, ignoring the protests of his friends, Julian rose and marched smartly over to the nearest guard.

'Now, listen,' he said. 'There's been a dreadful mis-understanding, and I think it's time we all put this nonsense behind us. My name is . . .' Julian couldn't help but notice the guard showed no sign of noticing him at all.

'Are you listening?' he hollered. 'HELLO?'

The guard was approximately nine foot tall, and appeared

to have been carved out of one of the harder, denser sorts of rock – possibly one that is used to cut other rocks.

'I see what you're doing,' Julian said, 'and I won't stand for it. For I'm a citizen of Britain, sir. Here – like many others – under false pretences. Or a miscarriage of justice. What's the phrase I want? Never mind. I shouldn't be here, is what I mean.'

He left a brief pause for reply.

Receiving none, he refused to be fazed. He went on, his back straight as a ramrod.

'I should be at home,' he said, 'eating crumpets drenched in butter and Gentleman's Relish, listening to Elgar or . . . or Gustav Holst – who was English, in fact – and reading Henry Fielding. I don't know if you've ever tried him. He really is terrific. Kingsley Amis agreed. Buried in Lisbon, of course.'

Julian couldn't help noticing that his hard negotiating technique (which didn't even work on coach-station attendants) had drifted somewhat into a more conversational stance. Without intending to, he seemed to have changed from Bad Cop to Good Cop – with both approaches falling on deaf ears.

He had started the conversation feeling as though he was

on the firmest of firm ground – which, in his mind, was Portland limestone. But now that ground suddenly seemed covered with bacon grease. Julian was starting to yearn for a reaction from the guard – any reaction.

He was about to observe that it must be terribly hard work, keeping a guard's uniform so impressively spic and span, and to wonder aloud whether he did that himself or if there was a Mrs Prison Guard who did it for him, and if that wasn't a sexist presumption, in this day and age, when he was arrested by a tap on the shoulder.

'It's no good, mate,' said Jim Clarke. 'They don't speak English.'

'What? None of them?'

Jim shook his head. 'Not a word among the lot of them. It must be a deliberate policy by prison management. The guards here are all Eastern European, at least as far as we call tell.'

'But what if an inmate needs medical assistance? What if someone has a genuine grievance? My God, we're not even supposed to *be* here!'

'Mate,' said Giles Reardon Smith, putting a sympathetic hand on his arm. 'Don't you understand? That's what everyone in prison says.'

'*Woof!*' *said Timmy.*
'*I knew you were going to say that, Timmy,*' *said Dick.*

Julian blithered silently for a few moments. And then it all got on top of him.

Perhaps it was the fact that he had gone without breakfast. Perhaps it was the prospect of an indefinite period stretching ahead of him without access to the products of Dark Star brewery, or to his own bookshelf. Perhaps it was because he knew he'd look a perfect ass in a yellow jumpsuit.

But he decided that, if he couldn't communicate with the guards verbally, he would find another way to make himself understood.

Turning to face the guard, Julian did his finest impersonation of a great ape in high rage. He jumped up and down, gibbering and hooting, and danced around making screeching noises. He waggled his bottom and slapped it in rhythm. He loped back and forth, mugging like his life depended on it, bending his legs and dragging his knuckles on the ground. He stuck his tongue out, blew raspberries and blubbered his lips with his waggling forefinger; he gurned and bulged his eyes; he pranced and cavorted like an unusually hungry gorilla whose last banana had been stolen by his least-favourite nephew.

At last, breathless and feeling rather glorious, Julian stood in front of the guard with his hands on his hips.

'You understood *that*, didn't you, you bloody self-importance ponce?' he said.

The guard remained entirely impassive.

Julian looked around, expecting to be greeted by a wave of applause from the other inmates. But, instead, he noticed that they had all retreated to the far corner of the yard and were looking at him with something like bare terror.

Then he felt a sharp pain on the back of his head, and everything went black.

CHAPTER SIX

A Confrontation with the Guv'nor

It was in the middle of the following day that Julian was released from solitary confinement. A door opened and he stumbled out into the yard, looking like a cartoon character who'd just had a bomb go off in his face. His hair was sticking out at all angles, he was mumbling to himself under his breath, and he tottered first in one direction, while looking in another, and then, a few steps later, reversed the equation.

'Julian!' said Anne, rushing forward.

They took him to the water fountain for a drink, and then got him sitting down and asked if he was all right. He cleared his throat and seemed to notice them all for the first time.

'How are you? How was it?' Dick asked.

'I would really, honestly struggle to recommend it,' Julian said.

'Those brutes!' Anne cried.

'Don't worry; it's over now,' Julian said, as his eyes

focused and he tried to neaten his hair. 'I'd rather not dwell on the experience, to be honest. How are things up here? I see you've avoided joining the yellow-jumpsuit gang, for now.'

George explained that there were no spare uniforms. More importantly, she pointed out the door to the sleeping areas, the eating chamber, and where the guards came and went.

'That seems to be the main administrative block, over there, with the offices,' she said. 'In fact, there's Rupert right bloody now!'

'Woof!' said Timmy.

They all jumped up and rushed over. Rupert could be seen walking through an enclosed glass walkway that crossed between two blocks. They shouted and waved, but apparently he couldn't hear them. Instead, he stopped and had a conversation with one of his minions for what seemed like an eternity, with them yelling unheeded all the while, until George got his attention by throwing one of her shoes against the glass.

'Easy, tiger,' said Julian. 'That sort of thing will get you put in the hole.'

Rupert turned sharply, but when he saw it was them, he

'Leave it to me,' Julian said. 'What we need here is a
bout of pretty hard negotiating, and I'm the man to do it.'

became thoughtful. He dismissed his employee and then put a hand up to his cousins, as if to say, 'Fear not; all shall be explained.' He marched out of sight and, shortly afterwards, a klaxon sounded across the prison yard. Then, one of the high-security doors in the wall clunked and sighed as its seal was released, and it came open.

Rupert stepped out. He seemed a little uncomfortable, which (the others thought) was the very least he should feel.

'Guys,' he said, 'I'm so very sorry about this.'

'Don't worry,' said Julian.

A host of violent and unpleasant remarks had come to mind, but Julian saw that there was too much at stake to give in to his temper. There were times when hard negotiation was needed, and times when oil must be spread on the waters. All they wanted was for this to be over.

'It doesn't matter, Rupert,' he said. 'We'll all be laughing about this by teatime. Just let us out . . .'

Julian stopped as he saw Rupert's expression grow more pained.

'Don't joke, Rupert,' he said. 'I like a joke as much as the next man. More, perhaps.' He thought for a moment. 'No, about the same, actually. But this is not the time. Just release us.'

'If it were up to me,' Rupert said, 'then, of course, I'd release you in an instant.'

Anne felt she was going to faint again, and leant on Dick's shoulder. He put his arm round her.

'You see, I own this land,' Rupert continued, 'but I don't run the facility. It belongs to Her Majesty's Immigration Office. Now, after looking for you for hours and hours yesterday—'

'*Rubbish*,' said George.

'—I'm *appalled* to find you in here. Owing to no fault of any of ours, you've ended up in a place which, technically, doesn't exist. This place does good, important work, I assure you – helping to keep our country safe.'

'*What* country?' asked George. 'We're not in any country!'

'Good point,' said Rupert. 'Whoever's paying, I suppose. Which reminds me – I take it you don't have your passports on you?'

'Maybe this is all some sort of reality TV show,' said Julian. 'Where are the cameras? I mean, this can't possibly be happening. Can it? From our own cousin?'

'I thought not,' Rupert said. 'Of course, I will make representations to the governing board that you be allowed to apply for a lawyer, and your lawyer, if appointed, may furnish the documents for you, which might begin your application process.'

'Just give us our phone call,' George said. They hadn't had the ghost of a signal since they entered the castle, and their phones had all been dead for more than a day anyway. 'This can all be cleared up by the end of the day. Mummy and Daddy only live a couple of miles away, and can bring my birth certificate—'

'Impossible, I'm afraid. It's simply not allowed. If you were a citizen inside a UK facility on British soil, then yes, of course, you'd have a phone call, and all sorts of rights. But, as undocumented persons, it's truly shocking how few rights you have. Seems terribly unfair, now I say it out loud. Makes me wonder if I should have allowed this place to exist at all. Too late now, I suppose.'

'But Rupert, for pity's sake,' said Anne, '*you* can vouch for us! You know who we are!'

'Of course I do, dear Anne, but that brings us to another sticky point. Owing to a series of legal cases, I have had to change my name, for the time being, to Alfonso Gutierrez. So you see my testimony is quite worthless.'

Rupert saw that his cousins were all wriggling with questions and objections, and perceived that, unless brought under control, this interview might take up his entire afternoon. 'I promise to do my best, try and pull a few strings. I'm so sorry that you're in here. It is ghastly, I do see that. It'll be over soon.'

Julian pretended to remain calm until Rupert turned his back. Then, all the pent-up fury unleashed itself and, letting out a kamikaze scream, he attempted a running, jumping, flying scissor-kick.

CHAPTER SEVEN

Light at the Beginning of the Tunnel

When he was released from solitary confinement for the second time, with a second walnut-sized lump on the back of his skull where a guard had dropped him, Julian looked even more haggard than before. But now he looked wily too.

Again, he allowed himself to be half-carried to the sleeping quarters and showered with attention and sympathy for as long as he felt was plausible, until he suddenly got bored of it and snapped back into his old self.

'During my time in there,' he said. 'I've been thinking. Oh, Anne, do stop crying! I'm fine. Besides, starvation feeds the mind. Free from booze, I have discovered the devastating mental acuity I always suspected of myself!'

'Humility too, I see,' said Dick.

'Shut up. Also, I've lost weight. Look at my waistband! I'm looking fantastic. But back to the first thing. What are we?' he asked.

The others looked at each other.

'Fucked,' said George.

'Woof!' said Timmy, who could not approve of such language.

'No,' Julian said. 'We're not that. We're *British*. Hey, look, get Jim Clarke and Giles and the others over here too. Listen, guys, the people holding us here might be employed by the UK government, but they haven't got an ounce of British pluck between them. We're going to show them.'

'I don't think you should show them your backside again,' said Dick. 'It didn't go so well, last time.'

'We're going to show them much more than that,' said Julian. 'We're going to *escape*.'

'Oh, Julian, how exciting,' said Anne.

'How?' George asked.

'We'll find a way. What do you think, guys? Worth a shot?'

Several of the other inmates had gathered round to listen. They nodded seriously.

'I'm up for it,' said Giles. 'I've got a spoon I stole from the lunch hall a few weeks ago.'

'That's a start,' said Julian.

George looked at the walls around them. Every stone in those walls was about the size of a Mini Cooper and

Julian now suddenly understood that, in his current position, he offered one of the easiest and juiciest targets in all the history of revenge-taking.

looked like it weighed about fifteen tonnes. And, looking out through the slits in the walls, they appeared to be about ten feet deep.

'I think we'll need more than a spoon,' she said.

'Woof!' said Timmy.

'I knew you were going to say that, Timmy,' said Dick.

They hadn't seen Julian like this for a long while. For the first time in years, they had something truly devious and nefarious to work against – and seemingly insurmountable odds.

Julian was fired up and filled with a sense of adventure, like the Julian of old. Anne, on the other hand, was sceptical about whether they could find a way to break out of this medieval fortress. But she reasoned that, with the prospect of being stuck in here indefinitely, even if they failed in the end, the idea of it would keep them distracted for the time being, and would kindle the precious flame of hope.

Julian divided up the tasks. Digging was to begin in the sleeping quarters, which were close to the outer wall. The precious spoon was to be used carefully, and in turns. Everyone was put on high alert for other tools that might come in handy.

At the end of each day, after lights out, they discussed their progress in the dark.

On day four, Julian learnt that three sockfuls of dirt had been removed from the ground underneath Dick's bed – all prisoners slept on the ground, on thin mattresses. These were distributed throughout the main yard in the traditional manner – by pouring them out through the trouser leg, while whistling and trying to look innocent.

'It makes the bed bloody uncomfortable to sleep, to be honest,' Dick said.

'Think of Blighty,' said Julian. 'And glory. And, er, well . . . when we get back to Britain – which is only a tennis ball's throw away, after all – I'll bung you fifty quid. Can't say fairer than that.'

'Will you buy me *Persona 5* on the PS4?' asked Dick.

'Yes. Fine. Whatever that means,' said Julian.

'All right then,' said Dick. 'But this digging really feels like it's doing something dodgy to my back. Besides which, I'm not sure we're really getting anywhere.'

'Why do you say that?'

'Well, it's a stone castle, isn't it? What we can scrape away with the spoon is only the mortar between the stones. We can only dislodge them.'

'Can you lads shut up?' asked a voice in the darkness.

Julian opened his mouth to protest, and to say something about Britain, and values, and hard negotiation. But, after his two days in the hole, he was in dire need of sleep. And Dick's words had disturbed him. He turned them over in his mind as he drifted off.

CHAPTER EIGHT

What Every British Citizen Knows

The next morning, the plans for the tunnel were interrupted by a shock announcement.

Shortly after breakfast, a voice declared through the PA that a team of inspectors had arrived at the facility and were going to give several of the inmates the British citizenship test. This was an essential part of determining whether they would be released and allowed to re-enter the UK legitimately. The prison was alive with speculation and excitement.

Less than an hour later, all prisoners were ordered to line up and wait to be admitted to the admin block for examination.

'Brilliant,' said Julian, as they were led down a corridor with cells leading off it. 'Thank God this is all over and we can return to our old lives!'

But George wasn't so sure. 'I've heard these tests are absurdly hard,' she said.

Julian LOLed. 'I'm as British as Cheshire cheese used to make Welsh rarebit, with a dollop of Cornish clotted cream followed by a slab of Scottish tablet! And something else from Northern Ireland!'

'Which sounds utterly revolting,' said George, as she and Julian were ordered to stop in front of their respective cells. 'Good luck in there.'

'Luck,' Julian scoffed, as he pushed open the door and made his way over to the chair. 'Me? Need luck? To prove I'm British?'

Then he saw his interviewer, and his blood ran cold.

He heard a girlish scream of horror from further down the corridor, followed by a yell of anger from the cell next door and the sound of Dick shouting, 'Oh my God!'

Julian added one and one and one and one together.

'I always knew you were a close-knit secret society,' he said to Peter of the Secret Seven, 'and I knew you worked together, but I didn't realize where. So here we are. You've been immigration officials all along, have you? It all falls into place.'

'It says, here, your name is "Undocumented",' Peter said. 'Tell me, is that . . . Iranian? Or perhaps from Afghanistan?'

Peter looked at Julian without the slightest glimmer of

recognition. This, despite the fact that they had known each other since childhood and had run into each other twice in the last year alone. The first time had been at a day of team-building exercises in a country hotel, and the second was at a beach-body contest on the Dorset coast.

On the latter occasion, the Secret Seven had come off most decidedly the worse, and, as he realized this, Julian now suddenly understood that, in his current position, he offered one of the easiest and juiciest targets in all the history of revenge-taking.

He gulped, and suddenly felt neither strong nor stable.

'My name is Julian Kirrin,' he said. 'In fact, Peter, I do believe we've met.'

Peter made no response to this, but applied himself to the paperwork in front of him.

'Let's begin the test,' he said. 'I have many applicants to get through today.'

'Fine. Good. I'm looking forward to it,' said Julian. 'I love talking about Britain because I'm so British, old bean.'

'Exactly what an enemy agent who longs to destroy the West would say,' said Peter.

'But also what an innocent person might say, who *did* love it?' suggested Julian. 'Surely?'

'You know, I've heard parakeets in the park utter longer
and more articulate sentences than you, and understand
them better, as well.'

Peter rested back in his chair and looked down his nose. 'I sense that you loathe democracy. You hate freedom. You despise the West's decadence. Am I right?'

'Loathe decadence?' Julian asked. '*Me*? I'm the poster boy for it, mate. Last week, I drank an entire bottle of Baileys and watched *Ghost Rider: Spirit of Vengeance* while soaking in a "Preposterously Plush"-branded orange-blossom-and-cassia-bark bath bomb. Which was Anne's birthday present, actually, but which I nicked. If you don't tell her, I won't. Ha. It doesn't get more decadent than that.'

There was a cold pause.

'That is totally unbelievable,' Peter said.

'It was,' said Julian. 'But, in many ways, I preferred it to the first *Ghost Rider* movie—'

Peter silenced him with an upheld hand.

'But, as you say . . .' said Julian. 'The quiz. The thing. Yes. Let's start.'

'What was Winston Churchill's middle name?' Peter asked.

Julian laughed. Then he remembered that laughter was not an appropriate response.

'Is that a real question? You're having me on.'

'What was Winston Churchill's middle name?' Peter said again.

Julian looked around the room. It was so featureless, so characterless and horrible. And, all of a sudden, it seemed to be growing smaller. 'I don't know,' he said. 'Bertram?'

'When did the farthing go out of circulation?'

'You mean I don't even get the answers?' Julian asked. 'What sort of quiz is this?'

'When did the f—'

'Okay, okay,' Julian said. He squeezed his thumbs against the veins in his temples, creating a painful throb that helped him focus. 'I don't know; I expect it was with the advent of decimalization, which was in about . . . 1971?'

'How many people serve on a jury in Scotland?'

'Eight,' said Julian, without thinking.

Because Peter was looking down at the sheet, Julian was able to size him up. Okay, he's bigger than me, and he works out, thought Julian. But, if I jump him now, I'll have the element of surprise, and it would be enormously satisfying. Because, if I fail this test, which it seems I am about to do with flying colours, it means I'm not allowed into the UK.

But it also means I've got nothing to lose . . .

There was a howl of anger from one of the other cells as George was presumably asked an impossibly difficult question.

Julian looked up, until the howl came to an end. Then he looked down, and found himself eye to eye with Peter.

'The British inventor Michael Faraday was born in which London borough?' Peter asked.

When the door in the side of the yard opened, and Julian was released from solitary confinement for the third time, he looked barely alive.

'What did they *do* to you in there?' Anne wailed.

'Nothing,' he mumbled. 'They never do. That's the problem. I was trapped with my own thoughts. It was horrible. I went over every argument I've ever lost and tried to come up with intelligent comebacks. But no matter how hard I tried, I still ended up losing them . . .'

'You poor little darling. Come here, come here. Dick, help me carry him.'

'Hullo, Timmy,' said Julian, weakly. 'Thank you; that's nice of you to lick my hand like that. You're a good sort of a dog, aren't you?'

'He's even being nice to Timmy,' said George. 'He must be delirious!'

They laid him down on his sleeping mattress, then knelt around him.

'Now, can we fetch you anything?' Anne asked.

'Are the guards out of earshot?' he asked feebly.

'Yes. I think so . . .' said Dick, checking over his shoulder. 'Yes. Definitely.'

'Good,' said Julian, excited, getting up on one elbow. 'Then get the guys; we've not got much time.'

'For what?' George asked.

Julian raised his hand. He was holding a set of keys.

'Escape!' he said.

CHAPTER NINE

Escape!

'How the hell did you get those?' asked Dick.

'Got thrown into solitary for fighting with Peter, didn't I?' Julian asked. 'A guard had to come in and separate us. Well, he slung me over his back and, as he did that, I snatched his keys.'

'But he must have noticed that in ten seconds flat,' said Anne. 'He's a guard, after all. He can't get by without keys.'

'This is where I added a little touch of my own personal genius,' said Julian, leaning back and bestowing upon these mere mortals a flash of his brilliant grin.

'God, he's already back to his old self,' said George. 'Even *three* days in solitary doesn't make him tolerable for long.'

'I'd stolen Peter's keys, hadn't I? Only, Peter won't have noticed straight away. And I'll bet, once he did find out, he was too proud to come back and admit to the prison staff what had happened.'

'So you did a switcheroo?' Dick asked.

'Sort of. I pretended to throw the guard's keys out of the window and into the English Channel. Whereas, instead, of course, I kept the guard's and threw Peter's – which was itself immensely satisfying.'

'How about the fight? Was there anything satisfying about that?' Dick asked.

'Well, I got a good punch into the side of his head, but that doesn't have much effect because it's not where he keeps his brain,' Julian said. 'So, while he was dazed, I instead went for a couple of playground manoeuvres. Pulled his hair a bit, pinched his neck and gave him a good Chinese burn.'

'Ooof,' said George. 'I hate that. Good work!'

There was a general easing of tension in the room, and a feeling that Julian had done right by his relatives. After all, each of them had had to sit through the appalling process of being given a next-to-impossible quiz on UK manners, morals and history by one of their bitterest rivals. Which they had all, of course, failed. It was a relief to know that Julian had got some revenge.

'Well *done*, mate,' said Dick, with the awkwardness any man feels when offering heartfelt congratulations to his brother.

'Okay,' George said. 'I'm willing to admit that
was mildly exciting. But that's enough. Time to go home.
I want some ice cream.'

'You're the best, bravest, cleverest stick that ever was,' said Anne.

'In fact,' said Julian, 'with all this starvation, I'm getting more sticklike by the day. Look at this waistband! But, hang on, I'm getting distracted. We need a plan. And I've just thought of one. Here is what we do . . .'

'Oh, look, Dick, I just found your brain on the floor,' George said, ambling up to him. She was holding up a small pebble about the size of a walnut.

'Eh?' he said.

'Yes, that's about what someone would say, who's got a pebble brain. Don't stretch yourself, mate.'

'What's up with you?' Dick said.

'Do you ever say words with more than one syllable?'

'Of course I do,' he said.

'Go on, then.'

'Bugger off,' he said.

'Stunning,' she said. 'You know, I've heard parakeets in the park utter longer and more articulate sentences than you, and understand them better, as well.'

Dick looked her up and down, and then spat on the floor.

'Say that again?' he asked.

Rather than repeat herself, George terminated the conversation by running at him and taking him in a rugby tackle.

Several of the men in the yard had been shouting to one or the other of them to leave off. Now that battle had commenced, thirty or forty men closed in and started arguing with their fists. Before any of the guards could make sense of what was happening, there was a mass brawl in the middle of the yard that had to be broken up with the attendance of multiple prison officers.

Everyone performed beautifully, and the activity kept them busy for just long enough to allow Julian to go around the yard, testing all the keys on the different doors.

In fact, his fellow inmates were so highly efficient and organised that, at the point Julian wanted to explore the area of the yard in which the fight was progressing, he whistled, and a bunch of them broke free of the melee and started fighting in a different corner, making the guards and everyone else move with them.

Julian knew from experience that there were not enough solitary-confinement cells to accommodate more than a few people at once, and with the guards unable to remember who had started the fight, no one was singled out. When they had the prisoners under control, after ten minutes, they made everyone queue up for lunch, on the principle that full (or at least less hollow) stomachs would impede pugilism.

'So, Jim and Giles,' said Julian. 'I think it's best if we leave you behind. It's too risky to take more than five of us. Is that okay with you guys?'

Jim and Giles nodded. 'Good luck,' they said.

Julian looked along the line of fellow prisoners and they all nodded too.

'Thanks,' he said. 'Of course, the second we're back in civilization, we'll get you out of here. We promise.'

They kept their heads down throughout lunch, and did everything in their power to look bored, and boring, and to attract no attention whatsoever. Then, when they were allowed out in the afternoon, in response to a signal from Julian, half a dozen of the inmates started a fight again.

This time, the guards' defences were up and every guard in sight swarmed around the fighters. At the very same moment, Julian took his small group to a door in the opposite corner of the yard, slipped the key in and turned it.

'Quickly,' he muttered, holding the door open. A few seconds later, they were all inside and Julian closed and locked the door behind them.

They were in a dark passage with some electrical light filtering along from the far end, where the castle had been modernized. Towards this end, though, there were no modern fittings at all, and a staircase descended into darkness. This, of course, was the direction that the group took.

They were breathless with excitement as they went down, hardly daring to whisper to one another. They were descending into a part of the dungeon that had been unexplored for decades – perhaps centuries. At the bottom of the staircase, they found a door, but this one required no lock and could just be pushed open.

Inside was a dank chamber, wet underfoot, lit by slits in the rock opposite. At the far corner, the castle was showing signs of damage, and part of the room had collapsed.

'Gosh, this is exciting,' said Anne.

'This place looks like your bedroom, Dick,' said George.

'You trying to start up the argument again?' Dick asked. 'I think I owe you one after that rugby tackle . . .'

'Shut your cakehole and keep moving,' said Julian. 'Escape first, petty arguments later.'

They moved some of the rubble aside as quietly as they could and found there was a hole through into a further chamber.

'There's a WOMAN prime minister?' Wally screamed.
'You've got a lot to catch up on, mate,' said Julian.

'That's too small for any of us to get through,' said Dick. 'Isn't it?'

They all looked at Anne, who was the tiniest of them. The hole was indeed small, and she wasn't at all sure she could squeeze through it. It was also craggy, and the edges were covered with some sort of green phosphorescent slime.

She looked at Julian, who had always been about twice her weight and width.

'I'll get through there easy-peasy,' he said, jumping forward. Thanks to his prison diet and the excitement of the moment, Julian was able to slide through almost with alacrity.

Encouraged, the others quickly followed suit and found themselves huddled on a platform of rock as they waited to get used to the darkness. They could clearly smell the sea, and they could feel the pounding of the waves on rocks not far away.

This chamber was in the very bowels of the castle, and very little of it was left. It might have been a cellar that had long ago collapsed. As their eyes adjusted, they saw that from the ledge where they stood was a drop of nearly twenty feet to a cave.

'Belt time,' said George. She, Dick and Julian formed

the belt rope, as before, and the group used it to descend. George came last again, with Timmy on her back once more.

Wiping her hands on her trousers, she looked up at where they had come from, satisfying herself that they were at last out of earshot of their captors.

'Okay,' George said. 'I'm willing to admit that was mildly exciting. But that's enough. Time to go home. I want some ice cream. Why are you all holding your hands up?'

'Because of this,' said a man, stepping out of the darkness, with a gun in his hand.

Timmy growled.

CHAPTER TEN

Marooned

'Seriously, mate,' said George, 'I've just been falsely imprisoned and made stateless, then forced to escape from a medieval dungeon with a dog on my back – *twice*, mind you – and I haven't had any clean underwear for nearly a week.'

'That's as maybe,' said the man with the gun.

'I don't care if it's as maybe,' said George. 'I haven't bloody finished. I'm also not in the mood to be held up at gunpoint by some weird, spindly little creep with an enormobeard that would make Gandalf look like a shaveling.'

'A shaveling is someone with a tonsured head, like a monk,' said Julian. 'I think you perhaps mean "young shaver" . . .'

'My point,' George went on, to the man with the gun, 'is that, if you want that thing shoved up your jacksie, then keep pointing it at me. Or you could shoot me, I suppose, if it is loaded and oiled, and if it works, which is highly unlikely, given its condition, and yours. But I'm not putting my bloody arms up.'

The man with the gun had clearly expected to take charge of the conversation. But now he seemed rather deflated.

He had big round eyes, a heavily lined face and a white beard that came almost down to his waist. All of a sudden, he seemed to grow self-conscious about pointing a gun at these strangers.

He cleared his throat, and nodded.

He put the gun down and massaged his neck, and then cleared his throat again.

'I think he's trying to speak,' said Dick.

'Uh-hum,' said the man, nodding. His voice, when it emerged, was whispery and distant, filled with little pops and scratches, like the audio track of an early talkie. 'Suppose I don't have to kill yer,' he said. 'But what yer doin' here?'

'We're escaping from this horrible place,' said Anne. 'We were being held here against our will.'

'What, the upstairs flat, as I call it?' the man said. 'The castle? It's been empty for decades. What they using it for now?'

'Eating people is naughty,' said Anne. 'You mustn't.*'*

'Detaining immigrants,' said Dick. 'From the European Union. Or *to* the European Union. We're not quite sure.'

'The European Union? That a new name for the EC?' the man asked. They all nodded. 'Ah, well,' he said, turning and leading them down through the cave, where the light was stronger and the sound of the waves louder. 'It's a difficult topic. Complicated. People get opinionated about things like that. It's about sovereignty, you see?'

'Escape first, talk about politics later!' said George.

But the man didn't seem to hear.

He had led them to a strange shack against the cave wall, built out of driftwood and dried seaweed. He seemed wiry and strong, and yet, in certain lights, incredibly ancient. They wondered how old he really was.

'You see, I brought myself down here back in the early seventies, when I heard we were going to join the EC. Couldn't stomach it. Not for me. Marooned from civilization, I was. And no matter what you say, no matter how hard you ask, I'm not coming back out. No, I'm not. Not old Wally. No, sir. I'll keep catching me shrimp and me kelp, and sitting in me little hut, where I'll live to be a hundred and three, but I'm not coming out – no matter what you say.'

'We've left the EU,' said Julian.

'Right, then,' said Wally, picking up his fishing rod. 'I'll be coming with you. I wonder how my Shirley's getting on. Where's the nearest pub, do you think?'

'It's not as easy as that,' said Julian. 'We need to get back to the mainland. Look at that swell, and those rocks. We can't wait for the tide to go out, because the guards will be on us, and we can't climb round to the other side of the island, which faces the mainland. We'll have to go the wet route. What have you got that we could float on? Making a raft could take hours . . .'

Wally reached up and took the roof off his hut with one hand. The three walls instantly fell away. All four pieces were roughly equal in size.

'I've been prepared for this moment for nearly forty years,' he said. 'I've got some twine around here somewhere. Tie 'em together and we've got a perfectly good raft.'

'Wally, you're a lifesaver!' said Julian.

'Woof!' said Timmy.

CHAPTER ELEVEN

Life on the Open Waves

'Tally ho, my hearties!' cried Julian, as they pushed away from the rocks. 'Shit! Is it supposed to do that?'

The first wave that came in picked the raft up and deposited it back on the rocks, where the flimsy structure groaned and twisted under the combined bodyweight of five people and a dog. There was a fair amount of screaming and tumbling around, and Dick and Anne just about grabbed Anne before she fell off into the swell. After a breathless few seconds they had all scrambled back to the safety of the rocks and were looking at the fragile craft with profound misgiving.

'Maybe we should push off from somewhere else?' Anne suggested.

'There is nowhere else,' said Julian. 'Besides, one more crash like that and we're sunk. Let's just time it well, and row our guts out!'

In the twenty minutes or so dedicated to the raft's creation, the group had explored Marooned Wally's collection of flotsam, looking for things to row with. They had come up with a cricket bat, an aircraft propeller, half an oar, a prosthetic leg and a length of plastic guttering. Their combined rowing power was not, therefore, remarkable.

However, with the threat of being thrown back on the rocks foremost in their minds, they presently climbed back aboard and cast off a second time. Rowing with all their might, and by good luck avoiding another forceful incoming wave, they were soon at sea.

'Heave! Ho! Strain every thew and sinew! Keep going!' yelled Julian, who was sporting by far the most impressive and exciting piece to be found in Wally's trove: a marine spyglass. It made him feel so important and powerful that he had it to his eye pretty much at all times. 'Hey guys, go that way. No, *that way* . . .'

But it was no good. From the furthest corner of the little castle island, the Dorset coast was visible barely half a mile away. However, no matter how hard Julian pointed at it, and how loudly he yelled, it just seemed to grow smaller.

'It's the current,' said Dick.

'It's impossible,' gasped Anne.

*'I suppose when people say that worse things happen
at sea, this is what they're talking about,' said George.*

'Why don't you bloody row as well, instead of telling everyone else what to do?' asked George.

'Mutiny, is it?' Julian asked. 'Say that again and, damn me, I'll have you flogged, sir!'

George rose to her feet and stood face to face with him.

'By which I mean, I, er, I dropped my prosthetic leg,' said Julian. 'Sorry. It must have had a greasy ankle.'

By now the crew had been rowing as hard as they could for next to an hour, and travelling in the opposite direction all the while – at some speed. At the revelation that their captain had dropped his oar, the others shipped theirs and flopped on the raft, exhausted.

'We're being carried out into the Channel,' said George.

'Looks like it,' agreed Anne.

'Did anyone bring any water?' Wally asked.

They all looked at each other in disbelief.

'Woof?' asked Timmy.

'Look!' said Anne. 'A bottle! And it looks like it has a message in it! Quickly, someone dive in and fetch it!'

The raft's crew had been growing somewhat lethargic, but Anne's words galvanized them. Dick stripped off his shirt and dived in, reached the bottle in six strong strokes, grabbed hold of it and turned for home. He climbed back on the raft with the unhesitating admiration of all his fellow sailors.

It fell to Anne, who had spotted it, to open the bottle. She held it upside down and shook it until the scroll of paper came out in her hands, then unfurled it delicately.

"'My darling Dorothea,'" she read. "'How I have longed for you all these years, trapped on this desert island.'" Anne gasped, looked at the others, and clutched the letter to her chest.

'Well, go on,' said George. 'Don't leave us hanging.'

"'Little can you have guessed that I survived the shipwreck after all. And there you are back in England, thinking of me as dead. I can hardly bear it. My only slender hope is that by some chance this bottle finds you and you are able to *come to my rescue!*'"

Here Anne broke off to do some light screaming and jumping up and down. When Dick and Julian shouted at her to get control of herself, she eventually did so, and then continued with the letter.

"'My coordinates are Latitude 30 degrees west, Longitude 41 degrees south. Please find me. Your loving Arnold. PS, don't marry Derek.'"

'Well,' Anne said, 'we can't get in the way of true love.

Let's send this on its way.' So saying, she put the message back in the bottle, reinserted the cork, and flung it back out to sea, where it landed with a hollow plonk.

'I can't help feeling that might have been written a long time ago, Anne,' said George. 'I don't really fancy their chances of getting together, to be honest.'

'I reckon Derek's in with a shot though,' said Julian.

The others agreed.

'That bloke's got no chance anyway,' said Wally. 'Those coordinates were plain wrong . . .'

Not long later Dick spotted something floating not far away and jumped in to swim after it. As he climbed back on to the craft they saw in his hand another bottle. And in it – another message!

'"My darling Dorothea,"' Dick read aloud. The others looked at each other, frowning. '"In the days since I sent my last message in its bottle, I have worried that I actually got the coordinates wrong. Here they are:"' Dick read them aloud. '"I am alive. Please come and rescue me. Your beloved Arnold. PS, steer clear of Derek."'

Although their emotions had been stirred by the first message, this one received a more muted response. Dick dutifully re-posted it into the sea, and sat once more.

Not long after, however, Julian spotted something not far away on the waves.

When Dick returned with a bottle in his hands for a third time, and held it up to show that it did indeed contain a little scroll of paper, this was not cheered, but rather regarded with circumspection. He handed the note to Julian.

"'My darling Dorothea,'" Julian read, "'after consulting my map once more I am convinced I was holding it the wrong way up all along. THESE are my true coordinates—" oh to hell with this man. He's a rank incompetent. Good luck to Derek, I say. Let's actually put this to a useful purpose . . .'

So saying, Julian scratched out the lovelorn Arnold's letter, and on the flipside wrote one addressed to the British police explaining all about Rupert's illegal Brexit Island, and what was happening there. They all signed it, and then flung it back to the waves, with a prayer that it might somehow, and in some way, help their friends still locked up inside.

Then there was nothing left for the raft's crew but to sit, and to wait for the hand that fate would deal them . . .

'Dear diary,' wrote Julian. 'It is impossible to keep track of time because our phones have stopped. Although, from

'Vultures,' said Julian, despairingly, pointing up to the sky.
'Look at them up there! Circling! Waiting for us to die!'
'That's a hang-glider,' said Anne.

the way the sun keeps going up and down, I suppose that we have probably been at sea for a full day and a half. It feels like ten times that.

'It is a treacherous business, trying to negotiate the high seas in nothing but a humble craft, and now, at last, I understand why discipline had to be so rigid in the old British navy. All it takes is for one person to despair and it spreads to all the others.

'The poor, benighted, weak-spirited folk with whom I share my craft are sure to crack under the pressure at any moment. I can feel the madness spreading among my crew, here on the HMS *Gillian Anderson*, and am watching these feeble creatures for any signs of murderous intent.'

'Julian, would you mind not saying all that shit out loud?' asked George. 'It's not really helpful.'

'My pencil's broken, hasn't it? So I'm trying memorize the captain's log.'

'Just think it, then. If you must,' said George.

'And we'd rather you didn't think it, either,' said Anne.

'Also, we didn't agree to the ship being called the HMS *Gillian Anderson*,' said Dick.

'It's a perfectly reasonable name. She was born in London and is one of our greatest exports. And, after Brexit, strong exports are exactly what we will need. What would you rather call it?'

'Just the *Raft*,' said George. 'Stop worrying about it.'

'Nobody suggest the *Theresa May* – even in jest,' Julian said. 'One use of the phrase "strong and stable" and we'll be under the waves in seconds.' Seeing Wally's confusion, Julian explained that Theresa May was the prime minister.

'There's a WOMAN prime minister?' Wally screamed.

'You've got a lot to catch up on, mate,' said Julian.

'If actresses are allowed, I wouldn't mind the HMS *Keira Knightley*,' said Anne. 'I like her.'

'She's entirely wooden,' said George, 'so I suppose it fits.'

'Oh, that's not fair. Not in her more recent roles,' said Anne. 'Like the one where she got spanked by Magneto in Vienna.'

'I think I'm getting delirious,' said Julian, wiping his brow. 'I keep imagining people saying nonsensical sentences. Where do you think we are, by now?'

Dick squinted against the sun. 'It's very odd. We haven't seen land for hours, but we keep being dragged on this current that moves like lightning. We could be hundreds of miles from where we started, by now.'

'Think where we'll end up,' said Julian. 'Some jungle

paradise, I expect. Naturally, the locals will recognize me as their new leader and we will begin an existence of happiness in the tropics, being fed exotic fruits and fanned with palm leaves. I suppose an island couldn't exist without beautiful, dusky maidens—'

'Shut up,' said George. 'At some point in the next twenty-four hours, we're obviously going to get run down by a bloody ferry, if we don't actually sink first. Which, to be honest, sounds like a blessed relief, if it means I don't have to listen to Captain A-hole any longer.'

'What if we drift to Ireland?' asked Dick. 'That would be good; the Guinness is better over there, and we can fix ourselves up with EU passports – Grandad was born in Dublin, you know. Think how useful that would be.'

'I don't mind admitting I still miss Henrik,' said Anne, remembering the handsome Swede she'd met a year ago, just before the Brexit vote. 'If we end up in the Eurozone, I'll charge my phone, give him a ring and he's come and fetch me. He's *disgustingly* rich and extremely chivalrous. I was furious that he left London after the referendum.'

'All I want,' said Wally, 'is to be in a pub having a pint of best. Do they still do best beer? And some pork scratchings. Do they still do pork scratchings?'

'Incredibly, they do,' said Dick.

'But that's all academic, for now,' said Julian. 'All we can do is wait for the wind to change, or our luck to change. Or, please god, for just *something* to change . . .'

'Woof . . .' said Timmy weakly.

CHAPTER TWELVE

Alive!

'Dick, dear old bean, I was wondering if you'd help me with something,' said Julian.

'Of course.'

'Come over here. Look. This will seem odd, but would you mind just smearing this mustard over your arm?'

'Why do you w—? Oh. Oops. Clumsy Julian. May I ask what this is in aid of?'

'Of course you may. I'm going to eat you. Not all of you, you understand; just the bits you can lose—'

'Julian, no! Get off him!' Anne and George rushed Julian, to get his gnashers away from Dick's forearm, out of which he was attempting to take a juicy, Whopper-sized bite. Once he had licked the mustard off his own arm, Dick joined them in pinning Julian down.

'What's *wrong* with you?' Anne asked.

'Don't kid yourselves,' Julian screamed. 'We were all

thinking it! Look at him – he's young, he's tender, he's bound to be full of nutrients . . .'

Anne and George avoided answering this charge directly, but just ordered Julian to be quiet. When he complied, and had repeated aloud that he promised not to be an annoying prat any longer, they let him go.

'Eating people is naughty,' said Anne. 'You *mustn't.*'

'I suppose when people say that worse things happen at sea, this is what they're talking about,' said George.

'But aren't we all going to go mad on this boat?' Julian asked. 'Can we survive? Can we hold back our primeval urges for much longer? After all, one of Dick's thighs alone could keep us going for a week . . . look at it . . .'

The others decided they weren't going to listen to any more of this. They huddled in the furthest corner of the raft and took it in turns to keep watch on Julian, in case he came close, with his fangs bared.

As morning turned to afternoon, and afternoon drifted towards evening, the sun beat down on their tiny craft and they leant against each other, dozing, heads lolling, and thinking of water.

'Vultures,' said Julian, despairingly, pointing up to the sky. 'Look at them up there! Circling! Waiting for us to die!'

'That's a hang-glider,' said Anne.

They returned to gloomy silence for a few minutes, until George's eye was caught by a suspicious movement. She thought she saw Julian doing something, and, hoping that she was wrong, she crept up behind him.

'Got you!' she shouted.

All of a sudden, everyone was awake, staring. Julian's expression was a mask of fear and embarrassment.

'Julian, how could you?' said George, holding up the bottle of yellow liquid. 'Oh, and it's *warm*, as well!'

The others looked like they would retch.

George raised the bottle to her nose and confirmed her suspicions. 'You managed to keep a cider hidden from us all this time, and wanted to drink it yourself! You bastard!'

Anne and Dick looked relieved.

'I often go out with a spare cider in my inside pocket. It's for emergencies – just such as this one, in fact!'

'But drinking alcohol's utterly stupid,' said Anne. 'It'll just dehydrate you more!'

'Doesn't taste that way,' said Julian. 'Tastes pretty— Hey, stop that! Give it back!'

Julian, Dick and George were suddenly in a pile in the

'Pardon, monsieur,' *Julian yelled.* 'Où est l'ambassade anglaise?'
'You what?' asked the bloke.

middle of the raft, all fighting over the bottle. Anne was trying desperately to pull them off one another, and Timmy was jumping around, barking his head off.

Then, suddenly, they all stopped, as the bottle fell out of their hands, bounced clunkily on the edge of the raft and fell into the sea.

Julian opened his mouth to scream, but no sound escaped.

Instead of sinking, the bottle was standing up, perfectly still. Cider foamed from its mouth.

Then they noticed the stillness of the raft, the utter lack of waves. And they saw they were surrounded by wet sand.

Dick quietly let go of Julian's collar and smoothed it back into place, while George embarrassedly did the same with the fistfuls of Dick's hair that she had been grappling. Julian looked out from among a tangle of limbs and fists, and began to feel he had been a little hasty, a few moments ago, when he had roared that the other two would feel 'the lash o' the cat'. Not least because there was no available cat with which to lash anyone or -thing.

Timmy jumped on to the beach and the others tentatively followed suit. Their legs were shaky as they felt dry land beneath their feet once more. They looked at each other, and then at the bottle – they could not be distracted from

Julian comforted this bewildered time traveller with a description of what a Wetherspoon's was. Wally seemed to like what he was hearing.

their thirst for long. As Julian reached down to grab it before the others, another big wave came in and sent them all tumbling over.

'Woof!' said Timmy, disappearing into the distance.

CHAPTER THIRTEEN

Landfall

'I wonder where we are,' said Julian, walking up the beach. There were children playing in the middle distance, and parents lying on towels. They were just too far away to make out what language they were speaking.

'South Africa?' Julian wondered. 'Sweden? Virginia?'

'It's perhaps a little bit more likely to be Europe, Julian,' said Dick.

As they came up the beach, they approached a young couple. The girl was lying on her front, reading a paperback through sunglasses, while the boy was assiduously applying sunblock to her back.

'*Pardon, monsieur,*' Julian yelled. '*Où est l'ambassade anglaise?*'

They didn't seem to hear.

Julian got much closer, then barked, '*Embajada inglesa?*'

The couple both turned to look at him.

'You what?' asked the bloke.

His girlfriend swivelled her neck round to get a squint at this stranger.

'Yer blockin' ma sun, mate!'

'What country are we in?' asked Julian. Fortuitously, he had stumbled across a couple of English tourists – but that hardly narrowed it down. They could be anywhere.

'He wants to know what country we're in,' said the lad to his girlfriend.

She let out a low, throaty chuckle then turned back and carried on with her book.

Further up the beach, they got the same response from a group of middle-aged women, and Julian began to have his suspicions. A look at the beach huts stretching into the distance added to his hunch, and the statue of George III at one end of the beach sealed the deal.

'Fine,' Julian said, when they had availed themselves of bottles of water from the nearest shop and sat on a bench, looking at the sand sculptures, and rehydrating. 'So we landed in Weymouth.'

'Wicked,' said Dick. 'Let's get some candyfloss . . .'

'Don't be ridiculous,' said Julian, 'we are adults who have undergone the severest privation. The last thing we need is candyfloss. Besides, look at those prices. Instead may I recommend a trip to the town's delightful Wetherspoon's? It's to be found near Weymouth's picturesque bascule bridge and exquisitely colourful waterfront, but, more importantly, it serves pints of Devil's Backbone for less than three quid?'

'Three POUNDS?' Wally bellowed. 'For a pint of *beer*?'

Julian comforted this bewildered time traveller with a description of what a Wetherspoon's was. Wally seemed to like what he was hearing. Meanwhile, the mention of alcohol stirred something in the others. As Julian gestured in the direction of the pub, they rose as one man and marched towards it, as though he were a general sending them into battle.

Julian flopped onto the bar with his debit card in hand, and prepared to make what might be the single largest order of his (or anyone's) lifetime. He wondered momentarily whether it would be quicker simply to point out the things on the menu that he would *not* be ordering.

'You can't bring that dog in here,' said the barman.

Julian stood up straight. He had come through much, and was not to be trifled with. A speech leapt into his head fully formed. It had to do with principles, and human rights; it had to do with dignity, standing up to tyranny,

'Nice work, George,' Julian conceded.
'Well, we can't rely on your bloody negotiation tactics,' said
George. 'I didn't want us to be turfed out into the street.'

and remaining strong and stable in the face of adversity. Of Blitz spirit, good old-fashioned British values, hard negotiation, and spunk. It was going to be one of the speeches of his life, delivered with both barrels of his considerable pomposity and self-righteousness. But George beat him to it.

'What? Who said that?' she asked, feeling the bar with her hands. 'Where am I?'

'Oh my god,' said the barman. 'I'm so sorry. Please. Let me find you a table.'

'Nice work, George,' Julian conceded when the barman had retreated.

'Well, we can't rely on your bloody negotiation tactics,' said George. 'I didn't want us to be turfed out into the street. Eh, Timmy?'

'*Woof,*' Timmy agreed.

'Hmm,' Julian said, 'Well, you're probably right. I might retire from hard negotiations from now on. After all . . .'

But the others weren't listening. They were already poring over the menu. In short order an enormous feast was requested and paid for, and not long after, it was delivered to their table.

As they ate, however, the whole group were aware that

they were, of course, now fugitives, liable to be rounded up by the security services at any minute. They were constantly glancing into the street, expecting to see an armed response unit moving into position.

Then George pointed at a telly in the corner.

'Look,' she said. 'I recognize those yellow jumpsuits!'

On screen, men were being bundled into vans. Many of them were, indeed, attired in the familiar yellow uniform. Then, as the camera moved, the castle became clearly visible in the background.

When the video stopped, a headline appeared over it:

ILLEGAL DETENTION CENTRE IN DORSET SHUT DOWN.

'So we're not going to get . . .' Anne said hesitatingly.

'Nabbed by the rozzers?' Julian asked. 'Apparently not!'

'I was *not* going to use the phrase "nabbed by the rozzers",' Anne said quietly.

They watched, agog, as the scrolling newsfeed gave them additional information. It seemed that the discovery of the detention centre had come from an anonymous tip-off.

'That might have been our message in a bottle!' said Anne.

It also quickly transpired that the inmates were regarded

'I want to get wrecked,' said George.
'To celebrate not getting wrecked,' said Julian.

LANDFALL

as being innocent of all crimes, and after being processed, would be returned to their families.

'Thank god,' said Dick, 'so the boys got out as well. Just like we promised.'

'That's a relief,' said Wally.

'"Owner of detention centre named as Alfonso Gut-ierrez."' George read from the screen, '"still at large." Bastard got away.'

'And that means we won't see Lily again any time soon,' said Anne sadly.

'It seems to me,' said Julian, in a somewhat different tone from the others, 'that nowhere on earth is there to be found a kinder, wiser, more gentle, honourable, generous, thoughtful or more beautiful tribe than behind the bar at Weymouth Wetherspoon's. I love those guys!'

'You're drunk,' said George.

'Not quite,' replied Julian, 'I am experiencing something incredibly rare for me: a genuinely well-earned pint of beer. Get the shots in, Anne.'

'I shall do no such thing,' said Anne. 'We should be thinking about getting home. The coaches go from near here. If my phone was working I could order an Ultrabus Thriftzone Saver thingy . . .'

'Balls to that,' said George. 'I want to get wrecked.'

'To celebrate *not* getting wrecked,' said Julian.

'Yeah, lighten up, Anne,' said Dick. 'There's a time for being responsible and a time for, er . . .' he sought for the right word. 'Not,' he said.

'Fine,' said Anne. 'I'll have a Jägerbomb. Anyone else?'

'That's the spirit!' said Julian.

'What's a Jägerbomb?' asked Wally.

'Wait and see,' said Julian, 'Yes, Anne, we'll have one both. In fact, Wally, there are a few surprises in store. You might want to brace yourself. Where to start. Dick, how would you explain the World Wide Web?'

'I'll go and help Anne at the bar,' said Dick.

'The World Wide Web is a network of potentially limitless connected computers, able to exchange information directly at lightning speeds, connecting people across the globe in the blink of an eye,' said Wally. Julian stared at him.

'How do you know that?'

'I was at school with this lad, Tim Berners-Lee. It was an idea of his that he was often banging on about. Clever bugger – I knew he'd go far, even then.'

'Blimey,' said Julian. 'You're better prepared for modern

life than I thought. Here, mate, have a sip of this.' So saying, he passed over a Jägerbomb.

Wally sipped it.

When the resulting scene had died down, and Wally was starting to feel quite himself again, and the carpet had been thoroughly swabbed, sanity of a sort returned to the table.

'Sorry about that,' Julian said. 'Let's take things in baby steps from now on.'

Wally was not quite up to replying verbally, but (still dabbing his eyes and the corners of his mouth with tissue) he nodded.

'There's so much to explain,' Julian said, toying with a beermat. Turning it over, he spotted a piece of trivia printed on the other side. 'Huh,' he said, 'So Churchill's middle name was Leonard. Who'd have thought. Well, we fought them on the beaches. Didn't we, Wally?'

Wally eyed him dubiously.

'Alright, we didn't fight them. But we ran away pretty bloody brilliantly, don't you think? We escaped, after all?'

'Aye, we escaped,' said Wally, taking a sip of water. 'I'll drink to that.'

'After all that,' said George, 'we managed to escape

'After all that,' said George, 'we managed to escape back to almost exactly where we were in the first bloody place.'
'Hurrah!' said Julian.

back to almost exactly where we were in the first bloody place.'

'Hurrah!' said Julian, holding his glass up. 'To escape!'

'Woof!' said Timmy.